Smoke

by

Alison Prince

Illustrated by Patrick Morgan

Published in 2005 in Great Britain by
Barrington Stoke Ltd, Sandeman House, Trunk's Close,
55 High Street, Edinburgh EH1 1SR
www.barringtonstoke.co.uk

ISBN 1-842993-39-9

Printed in Great Britain by Bell & Bain Ltd

A Note from the Author

I was on a train about a year ago and a man sitting near me got out to have a smoke on the platform. He told his two children to stay on the train, he'd be back soon.

This made me think, "What if the train went off without him? What would the children do?"

There are a lot of boring answers, of course. The ticket man might have looked after them. Their gran might have met them. It might have been fine. But if it wasn't fine, what then? Read the book to find out!

To anyone who has ever got in a real mess

Contents

Chapter 1
Train

I hate this train. I'm bored.

Mum's in hospital. She's having a baby soon, and they say she's got to rest.

Dad's a lorry driver, so he's away a lot. He said, "Dan, you and Helen are going to

Gran's. Mum will worry if you're on your own."

Gran lives in Glasgow. I don't want to go there. I could look after Helen. She's 10 and I'm 14. We're not babies.

Dad's car failed its MOT test, so we have to go by train. Dad's fed up because it's No Smoking. He smokes all the time, but he won't let me smoke. He won't let me have a mobile phone, either. He's mean.

We've been on this train for hours. I don't want to go to Glasgow. I want to stay in London with my mates.

We stop at a station.

"Good," says Dad. "I'm going for a smoke."

I'd like a smoke, too, but I don't tell Dad that.

Dad doesn't know about last night. My mate Jim works in a shop where they sell

cigarettes. He left the back window open, so we could go in and nick some. He said the shop-keeper was out, but he wasn't. He came down from the flat upstairs and caught us. The police came. They wrote our names down. Jim Begg. Dan Ford.

The shop-keeper told me, "I know your dad. I'll let you go this time."

The cops said, "Next time, son, you're in deep shit."

Dad's buying a paper, cigarette in his mouth. I hope the shop-keeper hasn't told him.

Helen says, "I wish Dad would stop smoking."

A whistle blows.

The train is moving!

Dad's running after the train, yelling and waving his arms. We've left him behind. I start to laugh.

Helen says, "Oh, no! Can't we stop the train?"

I'm still laughing.

"What are we going to *do*?" asks Helen.

"We don't need Dad," I say. "Gran will meet us. She rang last night."

Helen asks, "Will Dad be on the next train?"

I shake my head. "Don't know. He should have got me a mobile."

"He said it would cost him a fortune."

"That's stupid. I'd only talk to my mates."

"Like, all the time," says Helen.

The ticket man's got a phone. He says, "Are you the kids whose dad left the train at Preston?"

"Yes," says Helen. I was going to say no.

The ticket man asks me, "How old are you?"

"I'm 16." I kick Helen under the table to make her shut up. I look older than 14.

"Is someone meeting you?" he asks.

"Yes, our gran," says Helen.

"Right," says the man. "Any problems, let me know."

_____

It's raining even harder. Helen's reading. I hate reading, it's boring. The fields have lakes of water in them. The train has stopped, but we're not in a station. The ticket man says, "There's water on the line. We hope to get going soon."

There are sandwiches in Dad's bag. Good.

We were stuck there for ages. Now we're moving, very slowly. I'm so bored, I could go to sleep ...

Chapter 2
Glasgow

"Wake up," Helen says. "We're in Glasgow."

We get out of the train, with all the bags.

It's not night yet, but it's dark out there. And it's still raining. The lights are on. Our train was late, Gran must have been waiting ages.

Gran's not there.

I look all round the station.

Gran's not anywhere.

"She hasn't come," says Helen.

I don't know what to do.

I go and look out in the road. There's a guy selling mags.

"Big Issue," he yells. "Help the homeless." He looks about 16.

I give him a cigarette, and I have one, too.

His name is Ross. I tell him about Gran not being there to meet us.

"Come to my place if you like," Ross says. "It's a bit of a tip, but it's OK."

"Great," I say. "Thanks."

I go back for Helen.

She's not there. Where is she? Panic, panic.

She's at a phone box, with all the bags.

She says, "I rang home in case Dad had gone back there. And Mrs Bell from next door was there. She'd come in to feed the cat. She says we have to go to the police."

I say, "I met this guy called Ross. We can go to his place."

Helen asks, "Can't we go to the police?"

"No," I say.

Helen gives me the same sort of look that Mum gives me.

"OK," she says. "We'll wait here for Dad's train."

Then she grabs my arm. "Dan, *look*!"

The train times have gone from the big screen with lit-up letters. There's just one message.

I don't know what it says.

Helen starts to read the words, but they are too long.

A woman tells us what it says.

"The trains have all stopped because of water on the line," she says. "There's a bus service from Motherwell."

"From what?" I ask.

"Mother-well," she says, making two words of it like she was talking to an idiot. "It's a town."

She starts to tell us where Motherwell is. It sounds a long way off. Buses are slow.

Dad won't get here for ages.

"Come and meet Ross," I say to Helen. "He's OK. He's a mate." I need a mate in Glasgow.

Helen's not happy, but she comes with me.

Chapter 3
Ross

"I'm fed up with this rain," Ross says. "I'm going back to my place. Come if you like – it's not far."

Helen says, "We've got to wait here for Dad's bus. From this place called Motherwell."

"The Motherwell bus won't come here," Ross tells her. "It'll go to the bus station."

I ask, "Where's that?"

Ross points and says, "That way. About 10 minutes from here."

"Let's go there," says Helen.

"Dad won't be here for ages," I say. "We can go to Ross's place for a bit."

"It's up to you," says Ross. He walks away.

"Come on, Helen," I say. "We've got heaps of time to meet Dad."

"Are you sure?" says Helen.

"Sure, I'm sure. Grab a bag."

Ross takes us through a lot of streets, then goes into a dark doorway. We follow him up steep stairs to the top floor.

We're in a big, low room. A lot of people are lying on mattresses or camp beds, and some are standing round a kettle, making tea. It smells of cigarettes and old food, but I don't mind. It's a good place.

A man says, "I don't like kids here. What if the cops are looking for you?"

I don't like being called a kid. I say, "The cops don't know we're missing."

"Don't be stupid," he says. "The cops know everything."

I give him a cigarette, and Ross and I have one, too.

"Where are you from, anyway?" asks the man.

I tell him what's happened.

Helen listens, frowning. We go on talking.

Helen goes to the door. She says, "If you don't come right now, I'm going on my own."

I can't let her do that. Mum would kill me.

"Hang on," I say. "Don't be stupid. I'm coming."

Ross comes down the stairs with us.

He says, "Go back the way we came. The bus station is just past George Square."

"Thanks," I say. I wish he'd show us the way, but I can't ask. "See you."

"Yeah," says Ross. "Perhaps." And shuts the door.

Chapter 4
Bus

It's taken us ages to get here. We got lost all the time and had to ask people the way.

The bus station is full of people. No-one can tell us where to look for the Motherwell bus, but a man in uniform said it would

come to this bay. We're standing there, waiting.

A bus is coming in.

"Motherwell!" the man yells.

I can't see if Dad's inside – the windows are misted up. Helen and I watch till the last person gets out.

Dad's not there.

I look in through the door, but the bus is empty.

Helen is crying. I give her a hug. This is getting bad.

"Tell you what," I say, "we'll get some chips, OK?"

She nods and sniffs.

The snack bar in the bus station is full of people. We can't get in there. There's an Indian café across the road – we'll try that.

*****

I don't have much money. I get chips and tandoori sauce. Helen looks a bit better. There's a phone on the wall. I have a brilliant idea.

"We can try phoning Gran," I say.

Helen says, "We don't know her address."

"We know her name," I tell her. "Isabel MacFee. There can't be that many MacFees. We just need a phone book."

I ask the café lady. She's wearing a sari and a woolly cardigan. She gives me a phone book.

There are lots of MacFees. I start phoning. The first three are not Gran. The next one doesn't answer. The one after that is a machine with a man's voice on it. I'm running out of money. Two more don't answer. I try the last three. None of them is Gran.

Helen is crying again.

The café lady says, "You got problem?"

I tell her what's happened.

"Does your dad have mobile phone?" the lady asks.

"Yes, but I don't know the number," I say.

Then she says, "So you call someone who know his number, yes?"

Helen has stopped crying. "Mrs Bell!" she says. "She can get it from our house. It's by the phone – Mum can never remember it because it's so long."

We don't have Mrs Bell's number, but we get it from the phone directory.

Chapter 5
Mrs Bell

"DAN!" says Mrs Bell. "Where *are* you? Your dad is doing his nut. He's been phoning me all day."

"In Glasgow," I say. "In a café. Dad wasn't on the bus from Motherwell."

"He wasn't on any bus," says Mrs Bell. "He hired a car and drove to Glasgow, because it was quicker. You weren't at the train station, so he went to the bus station. You weren't there, either."

Helen is listening. She gives me one of her looks. I know what it means. *We missed Dad because we were at Ross's place. I told you we should go to the bus station.*

Mrs Bell says, "The police are looking for you. Your dad reported you missing."

I shut my eyes. This is getting bad.

"Your gran tripped over her cat and broke her hip," Mrs Bell goes on. "She was lying on the floor in her flat, she couldn't move. That's why she didn't meet you."

Helen gasps and says, "Oh, poor Gran!"

"Where is she?" I ask.

"In a hospital in Glasgow. Your dad phoned me from there, half an hour ago.

She's all right. Your dad said all her friends were there. It was quite a party."

I say, "Lucky old Gran." My day has not been a party.

Mrs Bell says, "Dan, you must phone your dad, he's frantic. I'll give you his mobile number. Got a pen?"

I haven't, but the café lady gives me one. I write down Dad's number and read it back.

"Good," says Mrs Bell.

Now I have to call Dad.

I don't know what he'll say.

"DAN!" says Dad, the same as Mrs Bell did. "Thank goodness for that, I've been worried sick. Is Helen with you? Are you both all right?"

I tell him we're fine, but he's talking again before I've finished.

———————————————————————

"Listen, Dan, your mum's just phoned. The baby's started coming. I've got to go back to London. I'll come and pick you up. Where *are* you, for goodness' sake?"

I tell him where the café is.

OK, he's mean, but I'll be glad to see him.

Chapter 6
Dad

We're on the motorway. It's still raining. Helen is asleep on the back seat.

I'm in the front, with Dad. I mustn't go to sleep. Dad told me, "Dan, it's your job to keep me awake." So I have to talk to him.

I don't know what to talk about. There's only one thing I want to ask. So I'll ask it.

"Does Mum know you got out of the train?"

Dad says, "I couldn't tell her, with the baby coming. She'd have been worried sick." He goes on, "She asked how you were. I said you were fine, but I didn't know if you were. It was a bad moment."

He goes on driving. He lights a cigarette. He's holding out the pack to me.

"Want one?" he asks.

He's never said that before. I go to take one – but I stop.

This whole stupid thing has been because Dad left the train to have a smoke. He's in such a mess, he can't even tell Mum. I hand the pack back.

"Thanks a lot," I say, "but I'm giving up."

"Go on?" He sounds amazed. "I wish I could."

"Mum would like it if you did," I say.

"I know," says Dad.

*****

We're at a motorway café, with muffins and hot chocolate.

Dad phones the hospital. He asks about Mum.

"Thanks," he says. "Give her my love."

He tells us, "The baby's not here yet, but they say Mum's doing well."

*****

We're back in the car. Helen's asleep again. I must keep Dad awake.

"Dad—" I say.

"Yes?"

"If I'd had a mobile phone—"

"You don't have to tell me," says Dad. "I know you think I'm mean. But mobiles mop up money if you use them all the time. And we're not exactly rolling in it."

He drives on for a bit, then he says, "I'll get you a phone. But you buy your own top-up cards. OK?"

"OK," I say. "Thanks."

I'm happy about that.

Dad says, "By the way, I know about your little run-in with the cops."

Oh, no.

"Jack phoned today," Dad goes on. "The shop-keeper."

He's not looking at me. He's driving on, looking at the road.

"You won't do it again," he says. "Will you?"

I shake my head. I want to say I'm sorry, but I can't say anything.

"And anyway," Dad says, "you're giving up. I wish I could."

We drive more miles. Dad fishes for another cigarette. He looks at me, then puts the pack back in his pocket.

I say, "I've got some mints." I got them in the Indian café, with the last of my money.

"Go on, then," says Dad.

I give him a mint. I have one, too.

Chapter 7
Sorted

There's a small cot by Mum's bed. The baby is asleep. She's got dark hair like Dad's.

"What's her name?" asks Helen.

"Isabel," says Mum. "After your gran."

We look at each other, and we laugh again. Now Dad's told her, it sounds such a stupid story.

"You're hopeless," Mum says. "It sounds as if Helen was the only one with any sense."

Helen smiles, of course.

Dad doesn't smile. He looks at me, and I look at him.

He says, "We got it sorted, though, between us. Didn't we, Dan?"

I find I'm smiling. He's not mean, really.

"Yeah," I say. "We did."

Barrington Stoke would like to thank all its readers for commenting on the manuscript before publication and in particular:

Liam Brennan

Nick Rees

Haydon Smith

Become a Consultant!

Would you like to give us feedback on our titles before they are published? Contact us at the address below – we'd love to hear from you!

Email: info@barringtonstoke.co.uk
Website: www.barringtonstoke.co.uk

If you loved this book, why don't you read ...

Luck

by

Alison Prince

ISBN 1-842991-99-X

NO LUCK 4 DALE!

Dale hates school. He has no luck with girls. He fights with his mum. So how did he get to be a hero?

You can order *Luck* directly from our website at
www.barringtonstoke.co.uk

If you loved this book, why don't you read ...
Torrent!
by
Bernard Ashley
ISBN 1-842991-96-5

RUN 4 YOUR LIFE!

Tod thinks he's going to die.
The dam's broken. He's trapped.
He must get to the bridge before it's
swept away! Who can save him
now?

You can order *Torrent!* directly from our website
at **www.barringtonstoke.co.uk**